The Fisherman and His Wife

The Fisherman and His Wife

A TALE FROM THE BROTHERS GRIMM
TRANSLATED BY RANDALL JARRELL
PICTURES BY Margot Zemach

A SUNBURST BOOK   FARRAR · STRAUS · GIROUX

For Charles and Iva   M.Z.

Pictures copyright © 1980 by Margot Zemach
All rights reserved
Library of Congress catalog card number: 79-3248
Published in Canada by Harper Collins*CanadaLtd*
Printed and bound in Mexico
First edition, 1980
Sunburst edition, 1987
Second printing, 1995

Once upon a time there were a fisherman and his wife who lived together on the seashore in a pigsty, and every day the man would go and fish. And he fished and fished.

So once he was sitting there with his line, and kept looking into the clear water. And he sat and sat.

Then his line went to the bottom, way down under, and when he pulled it in, there on it was a big flounder. Then the flounder said to him: "Now just listen to me, fisherman. I beg you, let me live. I'm not a regular flounder, I'm an enchanted prince. What good will it do you to kill me? I wouldn't taste right anyway. Put me back in the water and let me swim off."

"Ah," said the man, "you didn't need to go on about it as much as all that—a flounder that can talk I'd let swim off anyway." With that he put it back in the clear water, and the flounder went to the bottom and left behind it a long streak of blood. Then the fisherman stood up and went back to his wife in the pigsty.

"Husband," said the wife, "didn't you catch anything today?"

"No," said the man. "I did catch a flounder, but it said it was an enchanted prince, so I let it go."

"You mean you didn't wish for anything?" said the wife.

"No," said the man. "What do I want to wish for?"

"My goodness," said the wife, "it's all wrong to have to keep living in a pigsty like this, that stinks so and is so disgusting; you could have wished for a little cottage for us, anyway. Go on back and call to it. Tell it we want to have a little cottage. It'll surely do that."

"Ah," said the man, "what do I want to go back for?"

"Why," said the woman, "you caught it, and you let it swim off again; it'll surely do that. Go on right this minute." The man didn't really want to. Still, though, he didn't want to go against his wife, so he went on down to the sea.

When he got there the sea was all green and yellow and not nearly so clear any more. So he went and stood by it and said:

"Flounder, flounder in the sea,
Come to me, O come to me!
For my wife, good Ilsebill,
Wills not what I'd have her will."

Then the flounder came swimming up and said: "Well, what does she want then?"

"Ah," said the man, "I did catch you, so my wife says I ought to wish for something. She doesn't want to live in a pigsty any more; she'd like to have a cottage."

"Just go on back," said the flounder, "she's got it already."

Then the man went on home, and his wife wasn't sitting in the pigsty any more; but there stood a little cottage, and his wife was sitting in front of the door on a bench. Then his wife took him by the arm and said to him: "Just come on inside." Then they went on in, and inside the cottage there was a little hall, and a lovely little parlor and bedroom, with their bed in it, and a kitchen and pantry, all of the very best, with the finest sort of utensils hanging up in it, some tin and some brass, everything that ought to be there. And out behind there was a little yard, too, with hens and ducks and a little garden with vegetables and fruit trees. "See," said the wife, "isn't that nice?"

"Yes," said the man, "and let it stay that way; now we'll really be satisfied."

"We'll think about it," said the wife. Then they had a bite to eat and went to bed.

So things were fine for a week or two, then the wife said: "Listen, husband, this cottage is entirely too crowded, and the yard and the garden are just tiny; the flounder could perfectly well have given us a bigger house. Really I want to live in a great big stone castle: go on to the flounder, make it give us a castle."

"Ah, wife," said the man, "the cottage is plenty good enough. What do we want to live in a castle for?"

"Nonsense!" said the wife. "Just you go on, the flounder can always do that."

"No, wife," said the man, "the flounder's just given us the cottage. I don't want to go back again, it might make the flounder mad."

"Go on anyway," said the wife. "It can do it all right, it'll be glad to. Just you go on!"

The man's heart was heavy, he didn't want to. He said to himself, "This isn't right," but just the same he went.

When he came to the sea, the water was all violet and dark blue and gray and not so green and yellow any more, but it was still calm. Then he went and stood by it and said:

> "Flounder, flounder in the sea,
> Come to me, O come to me!
> For my wife, good Ilsebill,
> Wills not what I'd have her will."

"Well, what does she want then?" said the flounder.

"Ah," said the man, pretty much upset, "she wants to live in a big stone castle."

"Just go on back, she's standing in front of the door," said the flounder.

Then the man went on back and thought he was going home, but when he got there, there stood a great big stone palace, and his wife was standing on the steps about to go in; she took him by the hand and said, "Come on inside."

With that he went inside with her, and in the castle was a great big hall with a marble floor, and there were lots of servants, who opened the big doors, and the walls were all shiny and hung with beautiful tapestries, and in the rooms were chairs and tables all of pure gold, and crystal chandeliers were hanging from the ceiling, and all the rooms and chambers had carpets on the floor, and food and the very best wine were standing on all the tables, so that they almost broke under the weight. Behind the house was a big courtyard with stables for horses and cows, and the finest carriages; and there was a magnificent big garden besides, with the most beautiful flowers and fruit trees, and a park at least half a mile long, with deer and stags and hares and everything anyone could wish. Said the wife, "Now, isn't that fine?"

"Yes indeed," said the man, "and better let it stay that way, too—now we'll just live in this fine castle and be satisfied."

"We'll think about it," said the wife. "And now we'll sleep on it." With that they went to bed.

The next morning the wife woke up first. It was just day, and from her bed she looked out over the beautiful countryside that lay before her. The man was still stretching when she poked her elbow into his ribs and said: "Husband, get up and look out the window. Look, can't we be King over all that land? Go on to the flounder and tell him we want to be King."

"Ah, wife," said the man, "what do we want to be King for? I don't want to be King."

"Well," said the wife, "if you won't be King then I'll be King. Go on to the flounder; I want to be King."

"Ah, wife," said the man, "what do you want to be King for? I don't want to say that to the flounder."

"Why not?" said the woman. "Go on this minute, I've got to be King." Then the man went and was all upset that his wife wanted to be King. "It's not right, it just isn't right," thought the man. He didn't want to go, but just the same he went.

And when he got to the sea, the sea was all blackish gray and the water heaved
up from underneath and stank just terribly. Then he went and stood by it and said:

> "Flounder, flounder in the sea,
> Come to me, O come to me!
> For my wife, good Ilsebill,
> Wills not what I'd have her will."

"Well, what does she want then?" said the flounder.

"Ah," said the man, "she wants to be King."

"Just go on back, she is already," said the flounder.

Then the man went on back, and when he came to the palace, the castle had
got a lot bigger and had a great big tower with magnificent ornaments on it, and
sentinels were standing in front of the gate, and there were lots of soldiers and
drums and trumpets. And when he got inside the house, everything was made out
of marble and pure gold, and there were velvet hangings and big golden tassels.

Then the doors of the hall were opened, and there was the whole court, and his wife was sitting on a tall throne of gold and diamonds, and she had a great big golden crown on, and a scepter in her hand, made out of solid gold and covered with precious stones, and on both sides of her were standing six ladies-in-waiting in a row, every one of them a head shorter than the one before. Then he went and stood there and said: "Ah, wife, are you King now?"

"Yes," said the woman, "now I'm King." Then he just stood and looked at her, and when he'd looked at her that way a long time he said: "Ah, wife, how nice for you that you're King. Now we won't wish for another thing."

"No, husband," said the woman, and she was all excited, "the time just drags by. I can't stand it any longer. Go on to the flounder. I'm King, now I've got to be Emperor too."

"Ah, wife," said the man, "what do you want to be Emperor for?"

"Husband," said she, "go on to the flounder. I want to be Emperor."

"Ah, wife," said the man, "Emperors it can't make, I don't want to say that to the flounder; there's only one Emperor in the whole Empire. Emperors the flounder just can't make; it can't do it, it just can't do it."

"What!" said the woman, "I'm King, and you're my subject. Will you go on this minute! Go on this minute! If it can make Kings then it can make Emperors too. I want to be Emperor! Go on this minute!"

Then he had to go. But as the man went along, he got all frightened and thought to himself: "This gets worse and worse. Emperor is too shameless: at last the flounder is going to get sick of it."

With that he came to the sea. The sea was all black and thick, and began to boil up from underneath so that it threw up bubbles, and a whirlwind passed over it so that the water went round and round; and the man turned gray. Then he went and stood by it and said:

"Flounder, flounder in the sea,
Come to me, O come to me!
For my wife, good Ilsebill,
Wills not what I'd have her will."

"Well, what does she want then?" said the flounder.
"Ah, flounder," said he, "my wife wants to be Emperor."
"Just go on back," said the flounder, "she is already."

Then the man went back, and when he got there the whole castle was made out of polished marble, with alabaster figures and golden ornaments. Soldiers were marching up and down in front of the door, and blowing trumpets and beating on drums and kettledrums; and inside the house there were barons and counts and dukes going back and forth just as if they were servants.

They opened the doors for him, that were made out of solid gold. And when he went in, there sat his wife on a throne that was made out of one piece of gold and was at least two miles high; and she had on a great big golden crown that was three yards high and set with diamonds and carbuncles; in one hand she had the scepter and in the other the imperial apple, and on both sides of her, in two rows, were her life-guardsmen, each one smaller than the one before, from the biggest giant of all, who was two miles high, down to the littlest dwarf of all, who was just about as big as my little finger. And in front of her were standing lots of princes and dukes. Then the man went and stood among them and said: "Wife, are you Emperor now?"

"Yes," said she, "I'm Emperor."

Then he went and stood and took a good look at her, and when he'd looked at her that way a long time he said: "Ah, wife, how nice for you that you're Emperor."

"Husband," said she, "what are you standing there for? I'm Emperor now, but now I want to be Pope too. Go on to the flounder."

"Ah, wife," said the man, "what don't you want? You can't be Pope; in all Christendom there's only one Pope; it absolutely cannot make you Pope."

"Husband," said she, "I want to be Pope. Go on right away! This very day I've got to be Pope."

"No, wife," said the man, "I don't want to say that to it; this will never come to a good end; this is asking too much. The flounder can't make you Pope."

"Husband, what nonsense!" said the woman. "If it can make Emperors, then it can make Popes too. Go on this minute. I'm Emperor and you're my subject. Will you go on!"

Then he was frightened and went, but he felt all faint, and shivered and shook, and his knees and the calves of his legs trembled. And the wind blew over the land, and the clouds flew, and it got dark as night; the leaves fell from the trees, and the water surged and roared as if it were boiling, and the waves ran high and crashed down on the shore, and far off in the distance you could see ships firing distress signals and dancing up and plunging down on the waves. Yet in the middle of the sky there was still a little patch of blue, though all around on the horizon it was as red as though a tremendous thunderstorm were coming up. He went and stood there, all terrified and despairing, and said:

> "Flounder, flounder in the sea,
>   Come to me, O come to me!
>   For my wife, good Ilsebill,
>   Wills not what I'd have her will."

"Well, what does she want then?" said the flounder.
"Ah," said the man, "she wants to be Pope."
"Just go on back, she is already," said the flounder.

Then he went back, and when he got there, there was a great big church with nothing but palaces around it. Then he pushed his way through all the people, but inside everything was lit up with thousands upon thousands of candles, and his wife was all dressed in solid gold, and was sitting on a very much higher throne, and had three great big golden crowns on, and all around her was the greatest ecclesiastical pomp, and on both sides of her were standing two rows of candles, the biggest as thick and tall as the highest church tower, right down to the very smallest kitchen candle; and all the emperors and kings were on their knees before her, kissing her toe.

"Wife," said the man, and looked straight at her, "are you Pope now?"

"Yes," she said, "I'm Pope."

Then he went and stood and looked straight at her, and it was just as though he were looking into the bright sun. When he'd looked at her that way for a long time, he said: "Ah, wife, how nice for you that you're Pope."

But she sat there stiff as a poker, and didn't move or stir.

Then he said: "Wife, now be satisfied. Now you're Pope. Now you can't be any more."

"I'll think about it," said the woman. With that they both went to bed.

She wasn't satisfied, though. Her greed wouldn't let her sleep; she kept thinking every minute about what more she could be.

The man slept well and soundly—he'd walked a lot that day—but the woman just couldn't go to sleep, and threw herself from one side to the other the whole night through, and all the time she kept thinking what more she could be, but she just couldn't think of anything. As the sun was about to rise, and as she saw the red of dawn, she sat up in bed and stared straight out into it; and as she looked out the window, the sun came up. "Aha!" thought she, "couldn't I make the sun and the moon rise too?"

"Husband," said she, and poked him in the ribs with her elbow, "wake up, go to the flounder. I want to be like the good Lord."

The man was still half asleep, but it frightened him so that he fell out of bed. He thought he hadn't heard right, and rubbed his eyes and said: "Oh, wife, what are you saying?"

"Husband," said she, "if I can't make the sun and moon rise, and just have to watch the sun and moon rise, I won't be able to bear it. I'll never again have another hour of peace, as long as I can't make the sun rise myself." Then she looked at him so terribly that a shudder went over him: "Go on this minute! I want to be like the good Lord!"

"Oh, wife," said the man, and fell on his knees before her, "the flounder can't do that. He can make Popes and Emperors—I beg you, think it over and stay Pope." Then she got so angry and spiteful that the hair flew all over her head, she tore open her nightgown, and kicked him, and shrieked: "I can't stand it, I can't stand it any longer! Will you go on!"

Then he pulled on his trousers and ran off like a madman. But outside a storm was raging so that he could hardly keep his feet: the houses and the trees fell, and the mountains shook, and the rocks rolled into the sea, and the sky was all pitch black, and there was thunder and lightning, and the sea came in black waves as high as steeples and mountains, and all of them had on top crests of white foam. Then he shouted, and he couldn't hear his own words:

> "Flounder, flounder in the sea,
> Come to me, O come to me!
> For my wife, good Ilsebill,
> Wills not what I'd have her will."

"Well, what does she want then?" said the flounder.
"Ah," said he, "she wants to be like the good Lord."
"Just go on back, she's already sitting in the pigsty again."

And they're sitting there to this very day.